House on

Warbler Estates

by Afi Bhai

DORRANCE
PUBLISHING CO
EST. 1920
PITTSBURGH, PENNSYLVANIA 15238

Dorrance Publishing Co
585 Alpha Drive
Pittsburgh, PA 15238
Visit our website at *www.dorrancebookstore.com*

Interior Design by Tracy Reedy

ISBN: 978-1-4809-8533-9
eISBN: 978-1-4809-8514-8

I dedicate this book to the one and only God.

I would like to thank my parents for believing in me and investing their time and prayers for my success. Love you guys!

A special thanks to Lauren Wise for her contribution in editing this story. She is amazing at what she does and her input was immensely valuable.

1

It's a large custom-built house in a private gated community, standing alone on a vast empty lot. So far, this development is home to only a few houses, but that's expected to grow. Tonight, John walks around the house, shutting off all the lights before heading to bed. He navigates around countless moving boxes, his dog by his side as he heads down the hall to say goodnight to his daughter.

John pokes his head into his nine-year-old daughter's room.

"Good night, Angie. Sleep well."

"Hey, Dad, can we go into the pool tomorrow?" his daughter asks, putting down her book.

"Let's see how much we unpack tomorrow and then we will decide. We still have a lot to get done!" John says, his exhaustion overriding any desire to plan an outing.

"Okay, Dad. Good night," Angie says, attention already back on her book.

"Good night, baby . . . don't stay up too late," John says, leaving his daughter's door slightly open as he walks away. Once in the master bedroom, he attempts to usher his dog through the doggie door, which was built adjacent to the master bedroom's patio door.

"Go, boy . . . go outside and peepee . . ." Instead of heading outside, their Bull Terrier jumps up on the bottom side of the bed and lays down. John sighs. "Fine. You know where to go."

He climbs onto his side of the bed as his wife, Molly, comes out from the bathroom.

"All good, honey?" she asks.

"Yep," John responds wearily.

"Did you set the security alarm?" In a new house with no neighbors, Molly wanted to make sure they were secure.

"I did, honey, and I shut all the doors and lights, too," John reassures his wife.

"Thank you, honey! Let's get some sleep tonight . . . we have a lot of unpacking to do tomorrow." She climbs into bed next to her husband.

"Don't I know it. Good night, honey," John says, shutting off the light and leaning over to kiss his wife.

2

It's late into the night. The dog wakes up, slowly steps off the bed, and starts to walk towards the doggy door. As he gets a little closer to the patio door, he can see a shape sitting next to the doggie door. It appears to be a sleeping cat, but he knows that this is no real cat. The dog stops for a moment and whimpers before deciding to slowly move towards the doggy door again. As he closes in, the cat-like animal opens its eyes to reveal skinny, black pupils that slash vertically through bright yellow orbs. Almost instantly, the cat transforms into a huge, snarling monster, easily five times the size of the dog, who yelps loudly and jumps back into the bed, scared out of its mind.

John wakes up in a shock. "What the hell?"

"Oh my God, John! The dog is peeing in our bed . . . " Molly quickly feels the sheets getting wet and jumps out of bed. She turns the light on to show John she was right. The entire bed was covered in urine.

"What!" John struggles to shake the sleep from his mind.

"Scrappy, he peed all over in our bed," she says, pointing at the dog curled up on the bed.

A door slams shut on the other side of the house, startling both of them.

"Is there someone in the house . . . ?" she asks John, visibly scared.

"I turned the alarm on, though; how can there be?" But John hears the doubt in his own voice.

"Well, go check!" Molly urges him in a loud whisper.

Just then, the monitor turns on in the theater room. Molly shoots a frantic look at John, who walks quickly into his closet to grab his pistol and load it. As he is about to walk out, gun cocked, he hears his daughter scream.

Both parents quickly make their way across the hall towards Angie's room. Right outside her door, the sound of breaking glass rings out from the direction of the theater room.

"Check on Angie," John urges. "I'll go see who is over there." He swiftly moves down the hall towards the other side of the house. Molly bravely opens her daughter's door all the way, looking around in a full visual sweep before zeroing in on her daughter.

Her chest tight and heart pounding, she asks, "What's wrong, honey?"

"There is a clown in my closet," Angie says, voice cracking, her blanket clenched between her hands. She looks frozen with fear.

"What?" Molly asks in confusion, scanning the room again.

"I just saw a clown walk into my closet, Mom!" Angie repeats in a fearful whisper.

"Honey . . . ," Molly hesitates, thinking about the house noises. "That's not . . . possible, honey." Molly tries to think logically but is visibly shaking as she walks over to her daughter's closet. She knew there was no clown in that closet; clowns have been her daughter's biggest fear since she was a child. But then again, she's never seen Angie this scared, literally shivering, and the whole room seemed to be very cold.

Molly reaches out to open the closet door, revealing two large, black snakes flicking their forked tongues in and out, in and out. They both lunge at her simultaneously and cover her body as she falls down, screaming and yelling, trying to get them off her body.

John passes through the family room to get to the theater room, where the monitor of the theater screen has been turned on. The stations are changing randomly, like someone channel surfing. He glances around. The theater room isn't large, but on the couch, he can see an outline. In the screen light, John can tell that someone is sitting in one of the chairs.

"Who's there? I have a gun," he says with conviction, moving closer to the chair. As the figure begins to stand up, the TV flickers to a blue screen and John sees his greatest fear.

The massive eight-foot terror from his childhood stands before him: Freddy Krueger from the 1980's movies Nightmare on Elm Street. John stumbles backwards, firing three shots at the monster, but the bullets go right through his figure, like it was made of air. The bullets tore through the theater screen. John hears Molly screaming as the shots stop ringing in his ears, and he shouts out for them in response. Molly and his daughter come running to the kitchen, totally petrified. John calls out for the dog as they run to the

4

garage, and John scoops the animal off the floor before they all jump in one of the cars. John squeals out of the driveway and takes off in the street. As they pass by the front of the house, shadows flicker in the windows.

John dials a number from his cell phone. The call goes into voicemail.

"You have reached Erin Conners with Massive Real Estate, please leave a message, and I will get back to you as soon as possible . . ."

"We are not living at this house!" he screams into the phone, careening out of the gated community. "It's fucking haunted! The HOUSE is fucking haunted. We are going to a hotel right now and moving our stuff back out of there as soon as possible. I want my fucking deposit back!" Angie covers her ears as John finishes his call and slams the phone onto the middle console.

3

5 Weeks Later

Realtor Erin Conners stands in front of the house, waiting on her next showing. She watches as a mid-size SUV enters the gated community and drives up to the lonely house on the street. She glances at her expensive watch and taps a kitten-heel-clad tow on the pavement.

Her client, Amir Siraiki, parks the SUV in front of the house, behind Erin's red convertible Corvette, and he and his wife emerge from their vehicle. Erin smiles warmly at Amir as Sharon unbuckles their 11-month-old baby from the car seat in the back.

"Hi! I am Amir," Amir walks over to shake Erin's hand, "and that's my wife, Sharon White, and our daughter, Naya." Erin extends her hand to Sharon as well.

Just inside the living room window, two shadows lurk, peering outside.

The male shadow speaks in an Angelic language, "They never learn . . .," it says to the other one.

Amir looks around the yard, clearly impressed with the place. "Wow . . . this is a beautiful house!"

"Seriously, I am not sure if we can afford this," Sharon says with a chuckle.

"It is a beautiful house," Erin agrees. "And a great deal!"

"So, why is it marked down so much?" Amir asks with curiosity.

"Okay, I will be honest with you," Erin begins, wanting to be completely transparent with the couple. "Nobody wants to rent or buy this house. We cannot get anyone to be able to stay for more than a week. We have rented it out five times since it was built 18 months ago, and each time, the tenants leave in the middle of the night, screaming."

"Somebody murdered in this house or something?" Sharon asked, half-jokingly.

"No . . . nothing like that. It's just haunted. There are ghosts in there. Honestly, this house gives me the creeps during the day, so I can't imagine what the nights are like."

"We don't believe in ghosts, Ms. Erin—" Amir starts to say.

"You wouldn't say that if you talked to the people that tried to spend the nights here," Erin admits with concern. "At this point, I've almost given up on this place."

"Let me clarify," Amir says, clearing his throat. "We don't believe in ghosts or goblins, but we do believe there are other beings among us. They live among us in harmony."

"Not these ones apparently," Erin says, glancing at the house. "So, you can't say I didn't warn you. After the last time, we have built in a 30-day clause in case you decide not to stay. It just protects both parties this way."

"Well . . . let's go in and see the house," Sharon suggests, opening the front door. She looked around inside. "At this price, no 'ghost' is going to keep us away." She gives an air quote on the ghost. The family walks into the house and starts roaming around together, from room to room. The spirits are watching the new family from a distance with vague interest.

The female Spirit Zheera speaks first. "They feel different."

The male Spirit, Sheeshal, much thicker in smoke than Zheera, agrees. "They are stronger." Then he has a realization. "They are aware of us."

"Can they see us?" Zheera asks quizzically.

"No . . .," Sheeshal responds after a moment. "They are not that strong." They keep watching from a distance.

"Do you guys have dogs?" Erin asks Sharon.

"Yes, we do; we have three dogs. A Bull Mastiff, an English Mastiff, and a Golden Retriever...," Sharon tells Erin before she has a chance to ask.

"But they are going to be outside dogs," Amir quickly chimes in, looking at Sharon for approval. "With a baby . . . we cannot have three big dogs running around the house and all over the carpets."

"Yes, that is true," Sharon says in a bit of sad agreement. "As long as they are comfy and happy outside, it will be fine. It's better for Naya anyway at this age."

Erin nods enthusiastically. "As you can see, the outside patio and pool is beautiful. This is a gorgeous house."

The tour finishes with Amir and Sharon trailing behind Erin, speaking in hushed tones. As they walk outside, Amir looks at Erin.

"Well, looks like we are going to take it. Are you still okay with our move in date?"

"Absolutely!" Erin says, excited. "You can move as early as you want."

"Great! Send me the paperwork, and we'll be in business."

4

A few weeks later, yet another big moving truck sits in front of the house. Three guys haul boxes and furniture through the front door with Sharon giving directions in the main foyer.

"All the boxes labeled as 'books,' please take them in front of the entertainment center in the master bedroom," Sharon instructs two of the men.

As she walks by her daughter's bedroom, she peeks her head in and speaks in Spanish to the nanny watching Naya.

"Lupe, could you please set these books up in the entertainment center please? You can just bring Naya over in our room."

"Si Chren," Lupe was fairly new to them. She had been with them since Naya had turned three months old. Lupe was an older Mexican woman, a grandmother herself.

Sharon walks over to the garage to retrieve more boxes of books. As she is pulling out a case with three special books in them, Amir pulls into the driveway with their dogs.

"Are the back doors closed, babe?" he calls out to his wife.

"Yes, and the doggy door is closed, too, babe," she yells back, her arms full.

Amir lets the dogs into the backyard from the back gate and they run, ecstatic and energetic to explore new surroundings. Amir walks over and gives Sharon a kiss on the cheek and grabs a box from the car.

* * *

As Lupe stacks books up on the shelf, Sheeshal hovers around, looking closely at the titles. There are lot of books on the three major religions: Judaism, Christianity, and Islam.

"They are learned about the true word of God," he says, closely inspecting the books.

Zheera was standing over by the back door, looking at the dogs running around outside, sniffing and marking territories. "It's going to be harder to scare them away with dogs outside," she says, looking over.

Just then, both Sharon and Amir enter the room. Sharon walks over to the entertainment center and places the three books on the top shelf. Sheeshal moves around her to see what she was placing on there. The three books were the Torah, the Bible, and the Koran.

"We cannot scare them away that easily, regardless," Sheeshal informs Zheera, shaking his head. "They know His word. They believe in Him, they pray to Him, and they ONLY fear HIM." The stress in his voice is palpable, and they both disappear.

5

Both Sharon and Amir are sitting in front of the TV in the family room, Naya asleep in her mother's lap as she strokes her head gently.

"She's asleep . . . poor baby. Must be exhausted," Sharon says, her voice hushed, caressing her child.

"So am I, man. I could sleep for days!" Amir moans as he shuts off the TV. Sharon carefully stands and brings Naya to her room, placing her in the crib. Amir heads outside to check on the dogs and give them treats for the night. He meets Sharon back in the master bedroom, where they quickly turn off the lights and fall into a deep sleep.

A few hours later, they both wake up to Naya crying loudly. Amir turns the lights on as Sharon jumps out of bed to check on the girl. As Sharon opens her door, cold air seeps over her skin. She takes a small step into the room, and that's when she sees it.

It looks like a dragon, with large teeth, bright yellow eyes, and long tail wrapped around Naya's crib. The pointy end of its tail was swinging back and forth as it stared at Sharon. To Sharon, the dragon appears as a greenish, smoky, hollow outline, and almost immediately, she begins to recite the Lord's prayer aloud.

"Our Father, which art in heaven, hallowed be thy name, thy kingdom come . . ."

The dragon freezes upon hearing the prayer; at that moment, it seems just as scared of Sharon as she was of it. Sharon slowly walks up to her daughter's crib, the dragon's eyes following her every move. But the words suppress the dragon's actions, and its tail is no longer swinging. Sharon picks up Naya slowly and backs out of the room, finishing her prayer.

" . . .but deliver us from evil, for thine is the kingdom, the power, and the glory for ever and ever. Amen."

She closes the door behind her and walks back into her bedroom, Naya cradled in her arms. "There was a dragon wrapped around Naya's crib?" she says to her husband, a half-question, half-statement.

"What do you mean . . . like a lizard?" Amir appears a little unsettled. "Did you kill it?"

"Not a real dragon—it's what the realtor was talking about. The spirits?" Sharon reminds him, setting Naya on the bed between them. "There are other beings in this house, remember? What are we going to do about this?"

"They are going to have to learn to co-exist, just like they do everywhere else," Amir says casually.

"And if they don't, what are we going to do?"

"I don't know . . . we will figure it out," he responds tiredly. Just then, a door slams on the other side of the house. Amir shakes his head. "We'll focus on unpacking tomorrow morning, and I will talk to Ahsan about it and see what he says."

"That's right, aren't they coming over tomorrow?"

"Yeah, to check out the new place and help us unpack. Let's try to ignore any other noises and get some sleep."

Amir turns the lights off, and the family falls into a fitful sleep.

6

 Amir and Sharon are unpacking dishes in the kitchen when an incoming text message dings on Amir's phone.

"They are pulling in the gate," Amir tells his wife. The couple excitedly head out to their driveway through the garage and wait for Amir's sister, Seema, and her husband, Ahsan, to pull up. Both are physicians at local hospitals.

"Nice house, dude!" Seema says, bouncing out of the car.

"Thanks. Where are the kids?" Amir asks as they all hug and greet each other.

"At home with the nanny. They'll come by later, so we can help get some stuff done in the meantime. I brought you guys some bryani," Seema hands over the dish to Sharon.

"Did you see the game last night man?" Ahsan eagerly asks Amir; he was very much into sports and loved talking about basketball.

"It was freaking awesome!" Ahsan continues his usual rambling on about the basketball game the previous night as they walk into the house, but by the time they reach the kitchen, Ahsan has grown completely silent, alert, and aware. Amir notices the sudden change in Ahsan, but the girls don't seem to, and Sharon leads the small group on a house tour.

The Spirits notice the newcomer in their house, watching him from behind the walls.

"He is very strong," Sheeshal tells his partner.

"We need to get out of here, he might see us!" Zheera says with worry.

"Yes, this may be a problem for us . . .," Sheeshal agrees, and they both disappear out of Naya's bedroom window.

The tour ends back in the kitchen, and for the first time since stepping into the house, Ahsan speaks, "You guys may have a problem." He sounds concerned.

"What are you talking about?" For a moment, Sharon had forgotten about last night.

"Our Spirit problem . . .," Amir gently reminds her.

"Oh, yeah," Sharon says, contemplating. "According to the realtor, this house is haunted, which is why we got a great deal . . . and there is definitely a Spirit here. It was wrapped around all over Naya's crib last night. I had to take her out and have her sleep in our bed with us."

"There's not just one spirit . . . there's two," Ahsan tells them, looking around, " . . . and they have an animal of some sort . . . a feline type. That's what you probably saw wrapped around the crib."

"Have you seen them?" It was the appropriate question to ask, since he seemed to know so much already about them.

"No, but I am pretty sure. Have your dogs been barking a lot?" Ahsan asks.

"Yes, they go off sometimes, randomly for a few minutes, like they saw something. But then they stop after a few minutes," Sharon explains.

"But they never used to bark randomly like this," Amir chimes in.

"That's because they can see them. And I bet so can Naya at her age," Seema says as she picks up Naya.

"Well, it's probably a good thing you guys are keeping the dogs outside," Ahsan tells Amir and Sharon. "Otherwise they would be going crazy all the time. I am not sure if I like these guys; they seem aggressive."

"Is there anything we can do?" Amir asks him, glancing at his wife, then Naya.

"I will need some time after the sun goes down to see what's going on—that will give me a better idea of what to expect." The four look at each other and nod in agreement.

7

The sun is setting as everyone finishes up slices of pizza for dinner. Seema's three kids are there with their nanny, and as the kids play, the adults clean up. Seema calls out to the kids from the kitchen bar counter.

"Come on guys . . . it's getting late. We should head home." Then she looks at Ahsan. "Are you gonna stay a little bit longer?" He nods, and Seema gathers up the kids and leaves with the nanny in tow. Sharon sends Lupe home, too, for the night. As they wave goodbye, Ahsan asks Amir and Sharon to take Naya for a walk while he goes back into the house.

As he walks around, shutting off all the lights inside and out, he recites a prayer in Arabic. The last light he shuts off is in Naya's room, where he then places himself square in the middle of the room in total darkness. He continues to recite his prayer, slowly growing louder until his voice bounces off the walls.

After the prayer is complete, he says in Arabic, "I summon you to present yourself to me and tell me your intentions." Then he bows his head slightly and continues with his prayer, eyes half closed but moving rapidly under his eyelids.

Suddenly, the room grows cold and two spirits emerge in rage and anger. Sheeshal hovers close to Ahsan and snarls in Arabic, "YOU DARE SUMMON ME . . . BOY?" Zheera is right beside him, hissing.

Ahsan slowly stands up and continues to alternate between prayer and questions.

"What are your intentions here? Why are you openly revealing yourself?"

His questions anger Sheeshal. "That is none of your concern, BOY! I have laid claim to this place . . . it is ours now."

"This house was not built to serve your needs," Ahsan continues to speak to the Spirit in Arabic. "Co-exist peacefully or I command you to leave—" But before Ahsan can finish, Sheeshal attacks him in fury, grabbing him by the throat and lifting him slowly up in the air.

"I will dissolve your soul," he growls at Ahsan, who is struggling under excruciating pain as he feels Sheeshal's iron grip clench around what must be his soul.

Just then, a much larger and darker Spirit flashes straight down from the ceiling, pushing Sheeshal, along with Ahsan, down to the ground. The new Spirit growls at Sheeshal in the Angelic language, which Ahsan could not understand.

"This human is under my protection. Do not touch him ever again!"

Zheera recognizes this new Spirit.

"Abu Zan?!" she wails. "Why do you interfere with our existence!"

"Your existence is of no concern to me—but he is." Abu Zan turns towards Sheeshal. "You have been warned, Sheeshal."

Sheeshal, from the ground, looks up in anguish. "My council will hear about this."

"Do what you please otherwise . . . do not touch him!" Abu Zan points towards Ahsan before flying back up through the ceiling. Sheeshal and Zheera disappear as well, flying out through the window and leaving Ahsan on the floor, drenched in sweat. After a few minutes, Ahsan gets up off the floor and splashes cold water on his face in Naya's bathroom. He goes outside through the garage to find Amir, Sharon, and Naya sitting out in the front yard.

"So . . . what happened?" Amir asks as soon as he sees Ahsan emerge from the house. Ahsan just gives him a silent stare.

Remembering that Ahsan rarely talks about his experiences with spirits, unless absolutely necessary, Amir clears his throat. "Right . . . so, we good to go back in?"

"Yeah, you guys are good to go . . .," Ahsan says hesitantly. "I'm gonna go, too. Have Naya sleep with you guys."

"Oh, believe me, I intend to every night. Is everything going to be alright?" Sharon asks, slightly concerned.

"Oh, yeah, absolutely!" Ahsan tries to respond with ease to comfort the family. "They won't bother you. But your dogs will be very hyper tonight and may bark a lot. This is normal, okay? "

"Yeah, got it," Amir responds.

Ahsan gets into his car and drives away as the three of them head back into the house and close the garage.

8

It was close to midnight when Sheeshal's guests began to arrive. Most of them enter through Naya's window, freely roaming the house, except for the master bedroom. This sends the dogs into a barking frenzy; there are eight of them, too many for the dogs not to notice and consider them strangers in the house. While Sheeshal and Zheera reside in this house, each of the other spirits live in the other empty houses in Warbler Estates. Spirit Naruzu is the first to share his concerns with the group.

"You should have stayed with peace, Sheeshal. This is going to be a problem. Why are these sons of Adam so strong for you to call on all of us?"

"They are people of strong faith and are well read on all three holy books. The male has a companion he calls who is protected by Abu Zan," Sheeshal explains.

"Abu Zan?" Spirit Naruzu is surprised to hear this name. "We need to stay at peace until these people leave on their own then. We cannot pick a fight with Abu Zan."

"Together, we are stronger than Abu Zan!" Sheeshal insisted to the group. "And he won't be able to stop us once more of these houses are built."

"Stay in the low . . . irritate the family and annoy them, but don't push them to call upon others. They will leave on their own," Spirit Raki suggests to Sheeshal.

"Don't tell us how to take care of our business. Mind yourself," Zheera snaps, annoyed by Raki's comments.

Sheeshal shushes her to be quiet. "We will not jeopardize our plan, but I will find a way to get rid of them."

The group of Spirits agree, and each exit the house using Naya's bedroom window.

9

 The next morning, Amir empties out the last box and crushes it up.

"Well, that was the last box. We are officially unpacked!"

"I am glad we had the weekend to get this done in. There are cleaners coming tomorrow." Sharon is relieved that the unpacking is finally done.

"Great. They can clean all this mess up! Hey, you wanna go to the pool and cool off?" Amir hopes Naya will love this suggestion as well.

"Sure, babe, sounds like a good plan," Sharon says excitedly. "I can finally get some sun!"

"Oh, yeah! It's a good day for it," Amir says, imagining sipping a cold beer in the shade.

After changing Naya, the family goes outside to spend some much-needed relaxation time by the pool and to play with the dogs. The Spirits watch inside through the window, observing how much the family loves their dogs. Too bad the animals are always outside.

10

It was nighttime and all three family members are asleep in their beds. Sheeshal walks around the bed in the master bedroom and comes up next to Sharon, hovering around.

"What's up, babe?" Sharon asks, assuming Amir walked up to her side of the bed. Her eyes barely open.

"What, babe...?" Amir responds from the other side of her, startling Sharon. She jerks her head to look at Amir sleeping next to her and turns back to see who was standing on her other side, but it was gone. Sharon lets out a weary chuckle.

"Fantastic," she murmurs before drifting back to sleep.

The next morning, Sharon sits at the kitchen table, feeding Naya in a high chair. The front door opens, and Lupe walks in, causing the dogs to bark for a few moments.

"Hola, Chren," Lupe greets as she enters the kitchen.

"Hola, Lupe. Como estas?" Sharon replies.

"Todo bein, Chren," Lupe says cheerfully, going to put her stuff into the guest bedroom.

Sharon reminds Lupe that the cleaners are arriving that day and that she would like Lupe to show them where to clean—just the large areas but not closets or small spaces. After her instructions, Sharon grabs her purse, kisses Naya good bye, and leaves.

Just as Lupe finishes feeding Naya, the doorbell rings, causing the dogs to stir again. Lupe opens the door to find a couple that says they are the cleaning crew. As they walk in, the dogs barking turns into low growling; they obviously did not like these people.

Lupe shows the woman, Olga, around the house and instructs where to clean as the man, Igor, heads back to his van to retrieve the cleaning supplies. Before returning to Naya in the kitchen, Lupe mentions not to go in the closets.

But while cleaning the master bathroom, Igor has the itch to check out the master closet. He looks around to make sure the nanny isn't nearby and then opens the closet door. Sheeshal stands right next to the oblivious Igor as the cleaner begins snooping around in drawers. First, he finds panties and sniffs them perversely. He finds jewelry in other drawers, which he paws through and picks out a necklace, putting it in his pocket. Sheeshal watches with approval.

"We can use you to help us with our cause. You have the potential to be much more useful with the right touch . . .." Sheeshal whispers in Igor's ear, although the cleaning guy obviously cannot hear him.

The next drawer opened has a bunch of small boxes, and he opens one to find an expensive jewelry set. His eyes open wide with excitement, but he realizes he cannot take one just yet. He discovers the same type of jewelry sets in the other small boxes. After closing the drawers, he walks to the other side of the dressers to find several expensive watches on the husband's side of the closet. He inspects them and chooses one to steal, again, stuffing it in his pocket. Not wanting to leave the empty box behind, he shoves the watch box down the front of his pants, leaving a barely noticeable slight bulge. Then he ventures out to his van to hide the stolen items before returning to clean. Every time he walks by the windows where they can see him, the dogs growl furiously.

Sharon was sitting in the breakroom of her clinic, eating lunch with the office manager and one of their medical assistant.

"How's the new place?" Merrill, an older lady who has worked with Sharon for many years, asks.

"It's beautiful!" Sharon responds. "Finally, we have a pool again. We will have a get-together soon once we get fully settled . . . although we have a slight problem we are trying to still get used to."

"What's the problem?" Stacey asks, taking a bite of her salad.

"We seem to have a spirit problem there," Sharon shares her concern with two women.

"What do you mean, like the one in your other clinic?" Merrill asks.

"Yes, but we don't sleep there at night, so she is okay with us," Sharon made the distinction. "These ones in our house are more active at night, and we seem to have more than one at our new house."

"Oh my goodness . . . that's terrible!" Merrill says, genuinely feeling bad. "Why don't you talk to Father Montessori again and see if he can help?"

"I was thinking about that," Sharon responds. "But it's only been a couple of days. Maybe they will calm down." Well, at least that's what Sharon hoped would happen.

12

Olga is washing the dishes in the kitchen of their small apartment when Igor comes up from behind, grabbing her ass before showing her the necklace he stole from the house.

"Oh, it's beautiful!" Olga exclaims in Russian, before realizing it must be stolen. "Where did you get it?" she asks suspiciously.

"Don't worry about it, it's yours!" he says, looking away. "Just don't wear it to work, it's too nice for that," he says, evading any eye contact.

"You stole it from the house with the dogs, didn't you?" Olga is upset. "If you get caught, we will lose our jobs."

"Don't worry. I won't get caught," Igor says confidently. "They have plenty of stuff that I am sure they don't even remember they have. Alright? But I gotta go now. I will be back later." He wants to get out of there without having to answer any more questions. Once in his van, he drives out to a pawn shop just a few miles away. Igor walks in and shows the pawn shop owner the stolen watch.

"I will give you $800 for it," the man says after inspecting it for a few minutes.

"Are you joking? This is at least a $5,000 watch!" Igor acts as if his price is the most ridiculous thing he ever heard.

"What do you know about watches, huh? I will give you $1,100 for it," the owner concedes, attempting to hand it back to Igor. But Igor nods in disgust.

"Keep it. Rip me off, you cheap bastard." Igor looks around while the shop owner gets cash out. "What's this?" He grabs a small 3" wide and 6" long stick from the counter.

"It's a retractable baton." The man grabs it from Igor's hand and pulls on both ends to extend the baton into 3-foot stick. "It's solid as a rock. You can use it to crack skulls when you need it and then easily fit it into your pocket afterwards."

Igor plays with it for a second. "Great . . . I will take this, too."

"That's 300 bucks." The owner tries to take the payment from the stack in his hands before Igor grabs the cash, but Igor is too fast for him.

"Trust me," Igor says as he leaves the shop. "There is a lot more stuff coming your way."

13

 Amir and Sharon are sitting in the kitchen, drinking wine, when Ahsan and Seema walk in.

"What's up, guys?" Amir greets the couple. Seema heads to the fridge to grab a Gatorade and offers Ahsan a drink. The couple had just gone to the gym.

"How are things going at the house?" Seema asks curiously.

"It's been interesting, to say the least," Sharon tells them. "Doors close randomly at night, weird noises . . ."

"The TV shuts off while we are in the middle of watching it and turning on when we are not," Amir chimes in.

" . . . I see a guy in green underwear always walking through our bedroom at night," Sharon says with a laugh.

"We need to block their path from going in and out of the house," Ahsan interjects, still on the serious side.

"And where is that?" Amir asks.

"They mostly use Naya's bedroom window because it's the darkest part of the house from the front. And the tree in front of the window doesn't help either," Ahsan tells them.

Ahsan and Amir walk outside the house to take a look at the tree in front of Naya's window. Amir lights up a cigarette.

"So, what do we do?" he asks, taking a drag.

"You need to brighten this area," Ahsan points out. "Put up a couple of lights shining on the window and one big flood light pointing to the tree."

"You got it. I will get that set up tomorrow. Thanks, dude," Amir says gratefully. A few moments of chatting later, Amir finishes his cigarette and they both head inside.

The next day, Amir installs the lights in front of Naya's window: two lights pointing at the window and one flood light pointing at the tree, just like Ahsan suggested.

14

It's dark outside when Zheera returns to the house alone to see her entry way completely drenched in light. Even though she is a companion of Sheeshal, Zheera is not as powerful as him. She is still fairly young.

Zheera now has to use the other path from another window. The unfortunate part is that the other entrance is through the back patio opening, where the dogs like to sleep. She doesn't like these dogs—especially the one named Bambi. Most animals are complacent about their existence, but Bambi seems be much more protective of her owners, willing to take on beings not from the human world.

Zheera slowly moves towards the back of the house, and as soon as the dogs see her, they start barking at her movement. Lip, the golden retriever, moves away from the area once he realizes she's a spirit and lays down. However, Bambi and Chubby stand their ground, barking at Zheera. She tries to sneak by, but Bambi snaps at her. Spooked, Zheera manages to get inside, where Sheeshal sees how scared the dogs made her.

"A human animal cannot harm you, Zheera," Sheeshal admonishes. "You should not worry about the beings made of dust and matter."

"I know . . . but she scares me. She is very loyal to her family," says Zheera, looking back at Bambi through the patio window.

"She does not matter. She will be taught her lesson soon enough if she continues to announce our movements every time."

15

When the doorbell rings, Lupe opens the door to find Igor and Olga. Bambi's barks turn into growls upon seeing Igor. Lupe let them in, so they could start cleaning, and Lupe walks back to Naya's room to check on the baby.

Again, Igor finds himself in the master bathroom and takes the opportunity to go in the closet. This time, he takes a whole jewelry set, stuffing it in his pockets and the box down his pants in the back. Sheeshal stands beside him the whole time.

As Igor walks back into to the hallway, Bambi starts growling again. He steps out the front door and stashes the jewelry in the van, then grabs his baton and stuffs it in his pocket—just in case he needs it.

He goes back inside, so they can finish cleaning. Igor grabs the garbage to take outside from the laundry room. The last time was not a problem at all, since the dogs were in the backyard. But as he stepped out this time, Bambi is right there, startling him. The laundry door closes behind him, and Bambi is poised to attack, growling at Igor hard. He quickly takes the baton out of his pocket and extends it, hoping to scare her off. He couldn't have known that she won't attack without her owner's permission. Sheeshal, who is following Igor, sees an opportunity and partially takes control of Igor's hand, hitting Bambi square in the leg, cracking it in half. Bambi yelps in pain and limps away.

Igor doesn't know how it happened and why he hit the dog, but he is sure the bone is broken and now he needs to cover it up. He sees a large canopy umbrella and pushes it down to make it look like that may have fallen on Bambi's leg. Then he quickly retreats inside the house. He urges Olga to finish up after making sure no one saw Bambi getting hurt. They tell Lupe, who is still in Naya's room, that they are leaving.

Meanwhile, Sheeshal is watching Bambi limp around on three strong legs, still growling at them. With his arms, he commands his feline animal to jump on Bambi's back and attach herself onto her back. Bambi tries to jump up and down to fight this feline off her back, but with three legs and her weight, it isn't long before the other back leg cracks as well. Bambi falls down, whining in pain, and the feline jumps off her and returns to Sheeshal's side. Bambi's back legs are both now broken and now she is unable to move. Sheeshal and the feline disappear back into the house, and Sheeshal approaches Zheera, who was watching him.

"Now you can freely go in and out of the house from the back without that dog bothering you." Zheera does not approve of what Sheeshal did, but she remains quiet.

16

 Amir is driving when he gets the call from Sharon.

"Hey, babe. What's going on?"

Sharon cries over the phone. "Bambi is hurt. Lupe says she has a broken leg."

"What? How'd that happen? Where are you?" Questions fall out of his mouth.

"I am on my way home," Sharon responds. "And I don't know . . . she thinks the umbrella fell on her leg. She is in a lot of pain . . ."

"Okay, I will meet you at home. I will be there in 30 minutes," Amir comforts her. He hangs up, makes a U-turn, and hits the gas pedal.

17

At the Emergency Veterinarian Hospital, both Amir and Sharon sit in the exam room, Bambi is laying on the table while the doctor goes over the x-rays with the couple.

"You see, she broke her left leg here . . .," Dr. Shultz points at the x-ray. "It completely shattered her knee. The only reason the leg didn't fall is because of the skin. It's completely detached. The other leg is a tension fracture from too much weight on one leg in the back, and it broke."

"Oh my God . . . poor baby!" Sharon has tears in her eyes, looking at Bambi. "So, what are our options?"

"Well, it's a big decision," Dr. Shultz is cautious, "we would need to operate on both legs if you decide to go that route. She will need four metal plates, two in each leg." He points out where on the x-ray.

"How much are we talking about here?" Amir asks, knowing the cost won't be cheap.

"Well, that's the big decision. You guys are in medicine. So, with all said and done, each surgery will cost around $4,000," he responds, rubbing his chin. "With two surgeries, you are looking at a little over $8,000."

"$4,000 per leg?!" Amir is shocked.

Sharon doesn't want to give up. "It's okay . . . we can work that out. We can get one done now, and after that leg heals, we will worry about the other one."

"Actually . . .," Dr. Schultz interjects. "I would strongly recommend that you get both of them done at the same time. She will not heal properly with three legs because of how big she is. Like I said, it is a big decision. I will let you guys talk." He exits the exam room.

"What do you think?" Sharon asks as the doctor leaves the room. They are both standing next to Bambi, showering her with love and long strokes down her back. Sharon is visibly emotional about the situation, and Amir knows how much she loves her dogs. They are part of their family.

"It's a lot of money. I don't even think we have ten grand to be able to pay." Amir is very frustrated knowing they can't pay for both the surgeries, even if he wants to. The choice is either doing surgery on one leg at a time or to put her to sleep.

"We can pay for one leg and worry about the other later . . ."

"You heard what the vet said; we need to do both or it's not going to be worth it. She will just break it again." Amir is thinking out loud, "She is too young . . . she's only a baby. We need to do whatever we can to help her, even if we have to borrow money from someone. It's not her time yet!"

"I can ask my parents for money . . .," Sharon volunteers.

Amir thinks about it as he looks around. His eyes fall on a pamphlet for CareCredit.

"How about this?" Amir picks up the pamphlet and begins to read through it.

"Good idea . . . we could try it," Sharon sounds hopeful.

Amir calls the number from the CareCredit pamphlet and fills in an application over the phone outside the hospital. He gets approved for $5,000 immediately and runs back in to let Sharon know. They both inform the doctor that they will proceed with the surgery. Considering her condition, the doctor decides to keep her overnight to perform the surgery the next morning.

18

Amir and Sharon are sitting in the waiting room the next day, waiting for Bambi, when Amir asks Sharon if she thinks the dog's injury was an accident.

"I don't know . . . it feels weird," Sharon responds, after thinking about it for a moment.

"I don't think it was an accident," he says with a sigh.

"You know what? I have been thinking about calling Father Montessori. He helped me a lot with the AJ clinic . . . maybe he can help with the house." Sharon is completely frustrated with the situation and wanted to let Amir know that she might call him.

"That's not a bad idea. Let's see what he thinks," Amir agrees.

19

Sharon is sitting at the kitchen counter when her cell phone rings. "Hi, Father Montessori." There is a brief silence as she listens. "Yes, the gate code is 2311 pound. We are the first house you see across the way." As she hangs up, she can see his car from her window. She steps out the front door to greet Father Montessori as he pulls into the driveway. Upon hearing the phone call, Sheeshal moves across the hall to the window to watch the Cadillac sedan approach the house.

Two men get out of the car: Father Montessori and his young assistant, Thomas.

"He should not find us in here when he comes inside. We must go!" Sheeshal tells Zheera, who is standing behind him, also watching.

Father Montessori embraces Sharon with a warm hug. "You remember my assistant, Thomas." He nods to Thomas.

"Yes, of course," Sharon shakes his hand.

"So, what's going on here? Same as your clinic in Apache Junction?" Father Montessori is a jolly, kind-natured guy.

"No, Father. This seems much more serious. These spirits seem more aggressive," Sharon shares her concern as they walk up to the front door.

"Nonsense, child…most spirits live in harmony with us humans. God intended the universe that way." It was clear Father Montessori doesn't want to believe there is malice intended for her family. Sharon opens the front door to let Father Montessori and Thomas inside. The dogs start barking for just a moment and then the barking turns into a whine, a pleading whine like when Amir and Sharon return home from a long vacation. While the dogs have never met the man before, they seem to know him.

Father Montessori's demeanor completely changes as soon as he walks in the house, his attention turning completely on Bambi. He walks straight to the back patio door and opens it. Lip and Chubby, suddenly the politest dogs ever, stand up as he walks by, then lay back down. Father Montessori gently pets them both on the head and continues on to Bambi. He squats in front of her and pets her head as well. Whining a moment ago, now in his presence, Bambi grows completely quiet. They stare into each other's eyes for a moment, as if they are having a conversation. He sees the whole story in Bambi's eyes. Then Father Montessori stands up abruptly and walks back inside.

"I need you all to leave," he says to Sharon, very politely but sternly. "I will let you know when it will be okay to come back."

"Okay, Father . . .," Sharon obliges, nodding to Lupe to gather up Naya.

Father Montessori looks at Thomas and asks him to bring in his case from the car. Thomas steps outside to carry out his order while Sharon buckles Naya in her car seat, gets in the car with Lupe, and drives away.

"Have they left?" Father Montessori asks his assistant as he takes the case from him.

"Yes, Father. I saw them leave the compound," Thomas responds respectfully.

Father Montessori opens his case up and takes out his Bible. He looks around the house, grabs Thomas, and takes him to the center of the house. This happens to be the hallway by the family room and kitchen. Father Montessori opens the Bible to a specific scripture and asks Thomas to kneel, handing him the Bible.

"Start reading from here and don't stop until I tell you," Father Montessori orders. "Don't be bothered by what is around you. This is important: do not take your eyes off the Bible as your words need to be heard without pause."

Thomas starts to read the Bible as Father Montessori walks back over to his case and takes out a Catholic Thurible. He starts to recite a prayer in Latin, opens the top of the Thurible, and starts to put drops from random vials in his case into it. As soon as he puts the last drops into the Thurible, a steady stream of smoke emerges from the top of it, but there is no fire.

The smoke starts to wrap around Father Montessori as he continues to recite in Latin with his eyes closed. Once he is totally submerged in the smoke, he jerks his head once violently, as if trying to roll his eyes in their sockets.

Then he opens his eyes, still reciting in Latin. His eyesight has changed. He is now seeing in the same vision as the spirits do, through a dark, greenish smoke. Father Montessori can see within and through the house walls. He turns to look at Thomas, kneeling on the floor, still reading the Bible. Even he appears in green smoke, the words he is reading are being written out in the most beautiful neon teal color, flying right into the air.

Father Montessori looks at the Thurible, smoke pouring out from it. He grabs it and wraps the chain around his forearm while holding the Thurible in his hand. He starts to walk around the house, gently moving the Thurible back and forth in his right hand as he continues reciting in Latin. All of the smoke rising from the Thurible, spreading across the house.

He reaches the laundry room door, and as he gets closer, his gently swinging arm does a long extension, swinging up high and then coming back down. The smoke that comes up forms a shape of a seven-foot-tall smoke tiger. The tiger-shaped smoke takes its post in front of the laundry room door, and Father Montessori moves onto the hallway. With another long swing, the smoke creates another solider, this time in the shape of a hawk. He places a bull by the door leading to the garage, a bear in front of the back-patio door, and a gorilla beside the front door. He then moves into the master bedroom. By the patio door there, Father Montessori places a wolf, but before the wolf can take its post, it sees Sheeshal's feline hiding in the closet. Father Montessori sees it, too. The wolf swiftly moves towards and hits it with its smoke spear. The feline hisses with excruciating pain but manages to run past both of them into Naya's room and out her window. As soon as it jumps outside, it turns into a real hyena.

The wolf takes its post by the door. Father Montessori goes into Naya's bedroom and places a lion in front of that window to protect it. Then he turns back around and heads into the kitchen, past Thomas, and out the back-patio door. He once again squats in front of Bambi, while Lip and Chubby sit quietly beside him. Father Montessori starts to gather up some of the smoke into his hands, creating a sort of "snowball" while continuing to recite in Latin. Once he felt the smoke ball was big enough, he blows all of it in Bambi's face.

"I cannot heal you, nor can I take away your pain. But from this point on, no being shall ever be able to harm you," Father Montessori says to Bambi. Then he straightens up and walks back to stand right behind Thomas in the center of the room. He can still see the beautiful neon teal words coming out of the Bible. He looks up as he is praying and the smoke starts to rise and off him. Within a few seconds, it wraps around the whole perimeter of the house, creating a barrier.

As all the smoke leaves, Father Montessori closes his eyes again, and with a much lighter jerk of his head, corrects his vision back.

Instead of seeing the words come out of the Bible now, Father Montessori hears Thomas's voice instead. He places his hands on his Thomas's shoulders as an indicator for him to stop and realizes Thomas's shirt, face, and body is completely drenched in sweat.

"We are done here, son . . . you did good."

Thomas puts everything away in the case for Father Montessori, and they both head out of the house.

20

Later that afternoon, Amir and Sharon return to the house in separate cars. Lupe and Naya are with Sharon in her SUV, and Amir is driving separately in his car. They enter the gated community, and as they head down the street towards the house, they see a large, black hyena standing in an empty lot, staring at them as they pass by.

21

Amir and Sharon are sitting at the kitchen counter with Seema and Ahsan, drinking wine while the kids play outside with the dogs. They are laughing and having a good time—even Ahsan isn't feeling tense like he usually does at the house. He doesn't know why, but he also can't see the smoke soldiers standing guard at the house.

"Seems things are good in here?" Seema finally asks.

"Oh, yeah! It's been very peaceful since Father Montessori made a visit. No banging of doors or dogs barking randomly," Sharon sounds super happy.

"Yeah, it feels good in here. How's Bambi doing?" Ahsan asks.

"She is okay . . . surgery wasn't very successful," Sharon says with some difficulty. "The plates didn't settle in place correctly, according to the vet."

"She barely walks," Amir adds. "Only gets up to pee or poop."

"Are you guys still planning to have the party...?" Seema asks as she suddenly remembers.

"Yes, next Saturday. It should be fun," Sharon responds. "But I have so much to do to prepare!"

"Great! I am on call, but I will send the kids over earlier," Seema tells Sharon, "and I will be there as soon as I am done with rounds."

22

When the doorbell rings, Lupe is in Naya's room with the baby, putting away laundry. She lets Igor and Olga into the house for the weekly cleaning. Bambi sees them but doesn't get angry nor does she growl. All three dogs just stare at Igor.

Immediately upon entering the house, Igor starts to wave his hand in front of his face, like he is waving off a fly. He complains in Russian to Olga.

"Why is there so much smoke here?"

Olga ignores him and goes in the other direction while Igor walks into the master bedroom. But the smoke around him is getting thicker. Before he can make it to the door of the master bathroom, he drops the cleaning supplies to wave away the mass amount of smoke that surrounds his body. He falls to the ground and starts scrambling, hyperventilating loudly because he can't breathe. He starts to scream, rubbing his face and neck with his nails. Scratch marks start to become visible on his skin.

Olga runs in with Lupe on her heels, holding Naya. By the time Olga reaches Igor, his face is scratched up, blood dripping down his neck as he continues to scratch himself hard.

Olga asks him in Russian, "What's wrong, Igor! What's wrong?"

Panicking, Igor can't stop scratching and yells at Olga to get him out of the house. Olga grabs him from under his arms, but she barely has to lift him. He is half floating, as if someone is already carrying him. As soon Olga opens the door, Igor almost flies out as if he was thrown. He stumbles off the ground, almost running to his van, with Olga chasing him. She gets in the driver side, and Igor yells at her to drive away, blood still running down his face.

23

It's the day of the party, and a truck marked with the words Party Supplies arrives at the house, backing into the driveway as the hyena watches from a distance. Two guys get out of the truck and start to pull supplies out of the back. As the hyena is watching the house, he sees the Soldiers placed by Father Montessori begin to leave, one by one. As he sees the last one leave, the hyena walks over to the house and turns toward Naya's window. He jumps in through the window, and as he goes through, turns back into a smoky feline.

24

That evening, there are over a hundred people in the beautifully decorated house eating, drinking, and mingling. Outside, dozens of little lit candles create a beautiful ambiance as a local band plays music. There is a variety of food, ranging from Mexican to Indian to American, even a sushi chef making fresh custom sushi for the guests. Meanwhile, a bartender doles out drinks at the bar. The dogs lounge inside a closed gated area, so they won't bother the guests. There are three bouncy houses for the kids to play in with a few nannies sprinkled in, so the adults can enjoy themselves as well.

Sheeshal and Zheera arrive at the house, just as it's getting dark, to find many people in the house drinking and being sinful. But they aren't alone this time: they have four other spirits with them that look like Father Montessori's soldiers, except these aren't in shape of animals. They have blank faces and are more transparent than the two stronger counterparts.

Sheeshal and Zheera walk among the guests, feeling the humans' jealousy and envy for the hosts and their success. This pleases Sheeshal very much. A few hours later, the party ends. Lupe has put Naya to bed, and Amir and Sharon say goodbye to their last guests and close the door. They head to their room to change.

Sheeshal walks out to the patio, where most of the candles have burned out.

"It's time we kick them out for a few days," he says angrily. He takes the fire from one of the barely lit candles and sets it on the chair, lighting the chair on fire. With a huge burst, the flames start to get thicker and higher. The back patio's ceiling is made of wood; it would certainly bring the whole house down.

Amir stumbles a bit out of the bathroom; both he and Sharon had imbibed quite a few drinks.

"I'm going to get a couple of waters and let the dogs back in the yard," he tells Sharon. As he walks past the kitchen windows, he sees a huge ball of fire in the back patio.

"FIRE!" he yells out, hoping Sharon can hear him. He runs over to the kitchen sink and grabs a fire extinguisher from the bottom cabinet, then outside to the patio. Sharon comes running out behind him. Before he pulls the trigger out of the extinguisher to put the fire out, he stops. He looks closer at the fire and realizes that it is big enough that, not only should the ceiling have caught on fire already, but the other furniture next to the chair. It looks like the flames are contained within a ball and can't burn any higher.

"Put it out!" Sharon yells at Amir, not focusing on what her husband is seeing. Amir pulls the trigger and uses the entire extinguisher to put the flames out, covering the back patio in white, soapy foam.

Sheeshal cannot understand why the fire was contained in a hollow ball, but it infuriates him. He begins to spin around quickly, with his arms extending outward. Zheera and the other Spirits join in and start spinning around in the same fashion. Their spinning is so fast that it starts a windy wave around the house, and all the cups and glasses left behind by the guests start to fall over, spilling drinks and crashing glasses all over the floor. The wind blew so hard that even the glasses still hanging from the bar started breaking too.

Sharon and Amir watch in amazement as all the glasses and cups shatter on the floor. Within a few minutes, all the glasses are broken and there is glass all over inside the house. Sheeshal stops spinning around, causing the other Spirits to cease as well.

Confused and bewildered, Sharon and Amir are not sure what they just saw. After letting the dogs into the yard, they walk back to the bedroom where Naya was still soundly sleeping, and locked themselves in their rooms for the night.

25

Sharon and Amir both awaken unusually early the next morning, considering the exhaustion (and drinks) from the party the night before. Amir takes a long drink of water from the bottle on his night stand, while Sharon lay awake.

"I need a Gatorade . . .," she moans.

"I'll get it for you . . . how do you think it looks out there?" he asks her.

"Did that really happen last night?" She is not sure but was hoping she had dreamt it.

"What part—the fire or the glasses breaking?"

Sharon sighs and cradles Naya in her arms. The parents both get up, put on slippers, and walk into the hallway toward the kitchen. The house is truly a mess. Broken glass and plates are everywhere; it looks like a tornado had come through the house.

They open the back patio door and find the dogs happily wagging their tails. Even Bambi has managed to get up to come see them. They inspect the burnt chair and the extinguisher foam still everywhere.

"I am still amazed how these chairs and table didn't catch fire, too," Amir comments.

"And the ceiling . . . it should have caught fire as high as the flames were," Sharon says, looking up.

"We were lucky."

"We weren't lucky, something was protecting us," Sharon says confidently.

"I know," Amir agrees.

"What are we going to do now?"

"Let's go get some breakfast. The cleaning service is going to send somebody different to help clean today since the incident with the other guys," Amir suggests.

"Yes, we never talked about that either," Sharon reminds him.

"I know; let's go to breakfast and we'll talk about it there. I think I have an idea," he glances at Naya. "Is Lupe coming today?"

"Yeah. I asked her to come in case we needed some help. She should be here soon."

"Okay, I will get ready first, then you can," Amir tells Sharon and walks into the bathroom to shower.

26

Amir and Sharon are sitting at Denny's having breakfast. "I think we need to go further back," Amir says thoughtfully, then takes a bite of his eggs.

"What do you mean?"

Amir thinks about it a moment. "Remember when Ahsan told us that the older the Spirit, the more powerful it tends to be? I think Father Montessori helped a lot, but the Spirits in our house are older than Christianity."

"So, what are you saying—we need to contact a Rabbi?" Sharon knew exactly where he is headed with the conversation.

"Exactly!"

"We don't know any Rabbis . . . in fact, I don't know anyone from the Jewish faith," Sharon says as she thinks about it.

With a little caution in his voice, Amir asks, "What about Allen, Laura's brother?"

"Your ex-girlfriend, Laura?" Sharon isn't really thrilled to hear that Amir wants to contact his ex-girlfriend.

"Yeah. You remember her brother Allen? He was there when we had that party at your old house. He converted to Judaism."

"So, you want to contact your ex-girlfriend?" She seems irritated, but she is also irritated at the situation. They should do whatever it took to cleanse the household.

"No, I want to contact her brother. Come on now, babe; she's married with two kids. We need a Rabbi like you said."

"I suppose. Do you think he knows somebody that may be able to help with this kind of thing?"

"I am sure he does. He spends a lot of time at the synagogue from last I heard. I will text Laura today and find out his number."

27

 Amir pulls up into the parking lot of a beautiful synagogue. Allen is there to greet him, and they embrace in a hug.

"Man! It's been a long time . . . look at you!" Amir says. Allen is dressed in conservative clothing, wearing a white button down shirt with black pants and black coat. He has a kippah on as well.

"Well, you know. Gotta turn your life around sometime!" he replies, laughing

"Yeah. From one extreme to another, I guess," Amir says, laughing, too. "So, who are we talking to in there?"

"He is a good friend of my father-in-law. He is a Rabbi at this synagogue, and he also teaches in Spirits and Super Natural Beings at the American Jewish Center. He is well versed in the subject like you wanted."

"I think he is exactly the person we are looking for." Amir is relieved to know that hopefully this will be the right person to talk to.

They both walk in and Allen directs him towards the offices. He comes up to a door and knocks gently.

The Rabbi's assistant, Levi, opens the door for them and Amir and Allen walk in. There are two gentlemen in the room: Rabbi Yannis is sitting at his desk, and there is another older gentleman, Rabbi Meir, sitting on the couch beside Rabbi Yannis. Levi points them to sit in the two chairs in front of the Rabbi's desk.

Amir initiates the conversation. "Thank you so much, Rabbi Yannis, for seeing us. It is very gracious of you."

Rabbi Yannis is a middle-aged guy with a short, greying beard and thick glasses.

"I am not sure what it is that we can do for you?" It isn't really a question, but it isn't a statement either. It's as if he was trying to figure out Amir's intentions.

"We have Spirits in our house that are pretty aggressive. I am hoping you can help us with that," Amir continues.

"We do not involve ourselves in the matters of other beings. You should leave them alone."

"And they shouldn't involve themselves in our matters either, yet here we are at this cross road. They are deliberately showing themselves to humans in efforts to scare us off. The house is labeled as haunted because of them."

Rabbi Meir, quiet up until now, asks, "And why is it that you think we can help you?"

"Oh, I am very sure you can help us find out what they want. As I said, they are very aggressive." Amir is now sure he was talking to the right people.

There is a brief silence as the Rabbi looks at his assistant, who quickly walks over to his superior. He gently places a hand on Amir's shoulder.

"We will see what we can do, and I will get back to you."

Amir, seeing his cue to leave, gets up and thanks them all for their time. Then Allen and Amir walk out.

28

 Rabbi Yannis is sitting in his office in the dark, reciting prayers off his prayer beads, when he hears a knock. Rabbi Meir walks in slowly.

"So, what did you find out?" Rabbi Yannis asks him in Hebrew.

"We know him as Sheeshal. He has been around a very long time—since the time of Prophet Abraham, peace be upon him. He is very powerful," Rabbi Meir replies as he takes a seat near Rabbi Yannis.

"What's he doing here?"

"I do not know. I do know that he is building a legion."

"For what purpose?" Rabbi Yannis asks, looking up from his beads.

"I do not know. Something you may have to find out yourself directly."

"I agree. We shall go there tomorrow, and I will find out what this Sheeshal is up to."

"I will have Levi make the arrangements."

Then Rabbi Meir gets up to leave.

29

A black SUV pulls up to the gate of the community, and Levi enters the code and starts to drive in. Sheeshal sees the large SUV approaching.

"I don't like who is coming here . . . we need to go," Sheeshal announces. He is annoyed at the constant interruptions and having to leave this house. But before they can leave, two Spirits fly in and block Sheeshal's path. One of them speaks to him in Angelic language.

"You are not going anywhere. He needs to talk to you."

"I do not answer to you or him." There is anger in Sheeshal's voice.

"No. But you do need to show respect."

Rabbi Yannis, Rabbi Meir, and Levi all get out as Amir and Allen approach them. Without even a glance, Rabbi Yannis passes by them. Levi addresses Amir and Allen as the two Rabbis enter the house.

"They won't be in there long, but we would still appreciate if you guys left for some time," Levi requests. Amir and Allen both agree and head out while Levi takes a post outside. When Levi called Amir to make the arrangements for today, Amir made sure that no one was at the house.

Rabbi Yannis and Rabbi Meir find Sheeshal and the other Spirits in Naya's room. Rabbi Yannis notices the four soldiers and the feline in the house as well. He does not waste any time and goes straight to the point with Sheeshal.

Rabbi Yannis asks him in Hebrew, "What is your purpose here?"

"I do not answer to you," responds Sheeshal in Hebrew.

"You know very well I can find out anything I need to know, but I rather hear it from you," Rabbi Yannis was still speaking to him in Hebrew, but his tone was much harsher.

"What I do here is none of your concern!" Sheeshal thunders back.

"Why are you calling your legion here?" Father Yannis is persistent with his questions.

"So, you do know some things . . ."

It is surprising to Sheeshal that Rabbi Yannis already knows he is trying gather up troops at the Warbler Estates.

"To what end? What do you want from here?" Rabbi Yannis asks again.

"I am done here," Sheeshal growls, turning to leave. Two Spirits block his way.

Zheera and two other soldiers of Sheeshal come from behind and draw their smoky spears into the backs of Rabbi Yannis and Rabbi Meir's protectors. While the spirits are busy fighting, both Rabbis are reciting passages from the Torah. This starts to bother Sheeshal. He immediately turns his attention to the Rabbis and utters a few words in the Angelic language, throwing out two small balls of fire at Rabbi Yannis and Rabbi Meir. Both tallit on their shoulders catch on fire. Rabbi Yannis is quick to pull his off and throw it to the ground, but Rabbi Meir is not able to and his hair and shirt catch on fire. He falls to the floor and starts rolling around, and Rabbi Yannis quickly comes to his aid and helps put the fire out. Rabbi Yannis realizes that Rabbi Meir is badly burnt. Now he is really angry.

He puts his hands in his pocket and takes out a small vial filled with holy water. He lunges the bottle at Sheeshal, and right before the bottle hits the Spirit, Rabbi Yannis recites a phrase aloud to make the glass bottle explode.

Zheera sees Rabbi Yannis throw the small glass water bottle at Sheeshal, and she jumps in front of Sheeshal to block him from it. The bottle explodes right before it hits Zheera and all the holy water lands on her. She screams in pain, then evaporates into thin air. Sheeshal yells out for her—but there is nothing he can do. Zheera is gone. He turns around to see Rabbi Yannis grab ahold of Rabbi Meir and walk out of the house, almost carrying him out to the car. Sheeshal remains in the living room, shrouded in sadness over the loss of his protégé.

30

That night, both Amir and Sharon are sleeping in their bed with Naya between them when Sheeshal walks up to Sharon's side, holding the feline in his hand.

"You have taken one of mine, I will take one of yours!" He extends his arm out over Sharon's neck. "Go . . . make her pay for Zheera." The feline walks on his arm down onto Sharon's neck and wraps down around her spine.

Sharon wakes up the next day with a great deal of pain in her back. She rubs her neck vigorously.

"What's wrong, babe?" Amir asks, coming out of the bathroom.

"I don't know . . .," she responds, rubbing her back. "My neck and back hurts really bad. I must have slept on the wrong side or something."

"You want me to rub it for you?" Amir offers a message.

"No . . . you have to go to work and so do I. Besides, it doesn't feel like that kind of pain anyway."

"Okay, babe. Have one of the docs look at it," Amir suggests. "You look like you are in a lot of pain."

"That's a good idea, babe," she replies, heading into the bathroom to get ready for the day.

31

When Sharon gets home, she is in extreme pain, walking like she's carrying 300 pounds of weight on her shoulders.

"Hey, babe . . . in here," Amir calls out as he hears the door close behind Sharon.

"Hi," Sharon replies in agony.

"How'd it go? Did you get an MRI done?" Amir asks.

"I did," she replies, walking over into the office where Amir was sitting.

"Waiting on results now I guess?"

"No. Dr. Wright went over the images with me afterwards. He didn't see anything."

"Interesting," Amir says, not looking at Sharon.

"What's interesting about them not finding anything wrong with my back?" Sharon bit back a tone of anger and frustration.

"Well, I was talking to Ahsan about it, and he said the same thing, that they won't find anything on MRI scans."

"And how would he know that?"

"I don't know, but they want us to go over there for dinner tonight."

Reluctantly, Sharon agrees.

32

Amir pulls into a cul-de-sac and then into the driveway of a beautiful two-story house. After parking, Sharon is barely able to walk and struggles to get into the house. Ahsan and Seema come to greet them at the front entrance.

"Looks like you are in a lot of pain," Seema says sympathetically. Sharon can only nod.

"Come on; let's get her downstairs to the basement," Ahsan says, grabbing Sharon's arm.

"Why?" Amir asks, alarmed.

"Because she doesn't need medicine. She needs help."

Amir and Ahsan each wrap Sharon's arm around their waists and help her down the stairs to the furnished basement into a room in the corner. This is where Ahsan does most of his spiritual work. Amir remembers that Ahsan once briefly mentioned that there are different methods used to communicate with the spirits. And his method is through fire.

The large back room is fully carpeted with floor cushions scattered around, lit only by a dim, stand-alone lamp. Before entering the room, they remove their shoes. Ahsan helps Sharon sit on one of the cushions next to a floor table, then walks around to light seven candles around the room. Once all the candles are lit, he shuts off the light and comes to sit next to Sharon in front of his table, which has various stones on it.

Amir is standing in the corner, but Ahsan indicates for him to sit down and says in a low whisper, "If you hear any rattling or see anything run around in the room, don't be alarmed." Amir nods in understanding, and Ahsan also gives him a short prayer to recite over and over again.

Ahsan proceeds to light a few incense candles while reciting prayers in Arabic. He takes out two towels and a bowl from the table's drawer. Then he places one towel next to him and another next to Sharon. He adds the incense candles in the bowl and arranges three stones on top of the candles.

The final ingredient is a powder that he sprinkles on top of the stones. As soon as the sprinkles hit the lit cherry of the incense, it ignites in a small burst of flame but immediately dies down to a much smaller flame emitting a steady stream of smoke.

Ahsan continues to pray as the smoke becomes slightly thicker. Ahsan has Sharon turn her back towards him, towards the smoke, and Ahsan starts rubbing his hands in the smoke as if he's washing with it. With one hand, Ahsan rubs the smoke on Sharon's back, up and down. With the other hand, he grabs one of the hot stones and presses it against the top part of Sharon's back. She jolts slightly.

At first, Amir hears a whimper, most likely Sharon reacting to the hot stone, but soon he realizes it isn't her making the noise.

The fingers on Ahsan's other hand are pressed deep into Sharon's back, as if he has a hold of something. Tears start to pour down the faces of both Ahsan and Sharon, like they are in pain, but it isn't pain that is causing them to tear up. It is something else. Ahsan's right-hand pierces through Sharon's back, but with his other hand, he periodically wipes his face dry with the towel. At other times, he uses the stone to try and loosen the grip of the thing he is holding with his right hand.

Sharon realizes there is something holding onto her spine and she is in the same state as Ahsan, crying profusely. She, too, is wiping her face with the towel. Every time Ahsan touches the stone to Sharon's back, it loosens the feline's grip to Sharon's spine.

It takes at least a few minutes for Ahsan to pull the feline off, and Sharon feels immediate relief when it happens. Ahsan tries to hold on to it, but it is very slippery gets out of Ahsan's grip before running off.

33

 In the car on the way back home, Amir asks Sharon how she feels.

"Like 300 pounds have been lifted off my shoulders. I felt like my back was breaking," she replies with a relief.

"That's what it was trying to do, break your back."

"Well, things just got a lot more personal," Sharon says, a determined look on her face. "If they are going to try to kill me, I am going to kill them first."

"And how are we doing to that, you think?"

"I have an idea. I have been following this guy on social media for a while since I saw him on the Today show. He has a PhD in Eastern and Western religions and speaks several languages, including Hebrew, Latin, and Arabic. He has traveled through China, Taiwan, India; I mean, most of the places around the world. He is considered an expert in all religions, including Hinduism and Buddhism…"

"Sounds like you have done your research," Amir says after a moment.

"We need somebody that understands all the religions. I am going to contact him and see if he can help."

34

The door bell rings and the dogs start barking. Sharon opens the door to find Dr. Iris Swami, and she welcomes him in. He is a tall man in a suit and a top hat with a light beard and round spectacles. He looks much younger than Sharon expected. Amir tells the dogs to be quiet as he comes and greets Dr. Swami.

"Nice to meet you, Dr. Swami. That means a 'Hindu Teacher,' if I am not mistaken?" Amir says as he shakes his hand.

"Yes, that is correct."

"And then 'Iris,' being your first name, meaning 'eye of the Hindu Teacher,'" Amir continues.

"Very astute. That is correct as well!" Dr. Swami admits with a light chuckle. "Yes. I was born in Spain in a very Catholic household, but I grew up in India, where I learned a great deal about Hinduism. I did my undergraduate studies in England and my post-graduate studies in China and Taiwan. I also spent a lot of time in Oman and Jerusalem and published various papers on Islam and Judaism."

"Wow," Amir was impressed. "So . . . what did you conclude?"

"Conclusion about what?"

"Religion. Who is right?"

Dr. Swami chuckles again. "Well, no one religion is complete in itself." This took Amir back, "But I believe every religion brings a certain dynamic, and all together, we get the complete picture."

"Including religions that worship idols?" Amir asks curiously.

"Absolutely! I believe everything in this universe has energy. Even objects," he replies easily.

This grew some doubts within Amir on if this is the right guy for the job, but he knows Sharon is adamant that Dr. Swami can help.

Dr. Swami asks that Amir and the family leave him alone for a few hours, even spend the night somewhere else.

"Are you sure you want to do this alone at nighttime, Dr. Swami?" Amir asks. Sharon gives him a dirty look.

"The spirits are more active at nighttime, and I can deal with them better," he explains to Amir. "I will be gone way before sunrise, and you guys can come any time in the morning."

Amir and Sharon agree, and they pack up Naya—again—and leave Dr. Swami alone in the house.

35

Amir and Sharon return with Naya the next morning after spending a night in a hotel, only to find Dr. Swami's car still parked outside in the front.

"He's still here…?" Amir says quizzically.

"Maybe he fell asleep afterwards," Sharon suggests.

They walk into the house through the garage and call out for Dr. Swami, but there is no response. As they walk further in the house, they can hear a mumbling of sorts coming out of the guest bathroom. Slowly, they make their way into the guest room.

"What's that smell?" Sharon complains as they both cover their noses. The mumblings grow louder as they close in on the bathroom. Upon opening the door, they see Dr. Swami cowering in the corner of the bathroom, sitting completely naked in his own feces and urine. He seems to be hallucinating with fear, as if something is striking him repeatedly.

Sharon tries calling out to him a couple of times, but he is completely oblivious to his surroundings.

"Call 911!" Amir tells Sharon. "He needs to go to the hospital."

Shaken, they walk back outside to wait for the EMT.

"Poor guy … what happened?" Sharon questions with sorrow and frustration.

"I think we know very well what happened. 'Poor guy' is right," Amir responds.

"What are we going to do now?"

"Well, I think you had the right idea, but we just went about it the wrong way," Amir says, thinking hard.

"How so?"

"I don't think we need all the religions, but I think only Abrahamic religions, monotheistic religions of the book. And it's not a job for any one person. We may need one representing each one." Amir paces around the driveway. The ambulance arrives, and the couple leads them up to Dr. Swami. Minutes later, the medics transport him out in restraints.

"You think we need to get Ahsan, Father Montessori, and the Rabbi all together?" Sharon asks after the ambulance leaves. "What ever happened after Rabbi Yannis left the other day anyway?"

"Apparently, something big. According to Allen, the other Rabbi got badly burnt. He says Rabbi Yannis told him that it was a candle that lit his Tallit on fire but both of theirs were burnt. More went on here than he led Allen to believe, and it's time we find out what the hell is going on." Amir tightly holds Sharon's hand as they walk back in the house.

36

Amir sets up a meeting with the four at a local restaurant in a private room. Ahsan came with him, and the first one to arrive was Father Montessori. Within a few minutes, Rabbi Yannis arrives as well. After greeting one another, they let the server take their drink orders before getting into it.

Amir goes first. "I want to thank you all once again for getting together for this. As you have seen, we have a problem at my house and I want your help to get rid of it—these Spirits—"

"Sheeshal," Father Montessori tells Amir of his name for the first time.

"Sheeshal . . .? There is more than one, right?" Amir asks.

"Yes, Sheeshal." It was Rabbi Yannis' responds this time. "There were more than one at your house in the Warbler Estates, but not anymore, which is why he is really upset."

"I am assuming you had something to do with that. What is he doing in their house, and why are there other spirits in other houses at the estate?" Ahsan had little information on them and wants to know more about them.

"Sheeshal is a very old and powerful Spirit," Father Montessori responds. "With every house built at the estate, he calls another powerful spirit to occupy and build his legion."

"To what end?" Amir asks.

Rabbi Yannis takes a drink before speaking. "He wants to be seen and he wants to be heard. From what I have found out, he does not want to live in the shadows anymore, hiding from human beings. He wants to come out in the open."

"But that is God's will. Is he trying to defy God?" Amir asks, not very familiar with the subject.

"He is just looking for one small place in God's great universe. He, or God, won't get involved," Father Montessori says.

"Well, we shouldn't allow him to have that space, should we?" Amir questions.

"I thought about that question for a long time after my last encounter with Sheeshal," Rabbi Yannis says with some reluctance, "and I agree with you. We cannot have him start a war from our sector. But I cannot defeat him alone."

"Which is why I asked the three of you to come together," Amir jumps in. "The three of you rattled him individually. Maybe you can get rid of him working together . . ."

Rabbi Yannis looks at Father Montessori with much respect.

"I like what you did with their dog..."

"Bambi?" Amir interrupts, "What about Bambi?"

Rabbi Yannis ignores Amir and continues to talk to Father Montessori. "Do you work with all the Spirits of Noah's Arc?" Father Montessori nods his head. "It worked well! Can you call them in pairs?"

Father Montessori nods his head once again. "This time, I will, if we are to face Sheeshal and his legion. A male and female pair is stronger than ten men put together."

Rabbi Yannis turns his attention towards Ahsan. "And you—how did you come under the protection of a Spirit like Abu Zan?"

Ahsan didn't want to get into too much detail with them.

"I have been blessed, I suppose," he merely says.

"Good. Well, we will need his help," says Rabbi Yannis. "We will need you there as well." He looks at Amir.

"Me? Why me?" Amir is taken back by Rabbi Yannis. "I can't help in any way."

"I am not sure, but there is something between you and Sheeshal. He doesn't want to harm you for one reason or another," Rabbi Yannis explains to the group. "Which is why he attacked your wife instead of you."

Amir doesn't want to argue with this crowd, so he simply nods in agreement. "When are you planning to do this?"

"We should do it soon, and we should do it at night. We will hurt him the most when he is in full power himself," Father Montessori suggests.

"Yes, you are right," Rabbi Yannis agrees. "I can be ready as soon as tomorrow night." Father Montessori and Ahsan went on to agree as well.

"I will make sure Sharon and Naya are gone."

"We will need to strategize a plan, he will see us coming," Father Montessori says with concern.

"Yes, and he will be prepared to make a stand. We will work out the final details before heading in. Amir will coordinate the times tomorrow," Rabbi Yannis confirmed.

"I would be happy to," Amir replies

37

It is close to midnight, and three cars are parked at the gate to the Warbler Estates. They are all in their traditional, religious clothing, ready for battle. Ahsan is carrying his prayer beads, Father Montessori has his Thurible, and Rabbi Yannis has his holy water in his pocket. Amir had simply walked over to the gate after saying good bye to Sharon and Naya.

"He is expecting us," Father Montessori shares his concern with the group.

"Yes, and he is not alone in there. Everyone ready for this?" asks Rabbi Yannis.

"As we'll ever be," Ahsan responds.

As they all walk in through the side gate, they start praying. Ahsan prays in Arabic on his beads, Father Montessori swings his Thurible back and forth slowly as he prays in Latin, and Rabbi Yannis prays in Hebrew. They group slowly makes their way up to the house.

Sheeshal, watching from the window, sees them walk up. First, he sees the Spirit of Abu Zan join the parade, and then one by one, a pair of animal Spirits of Noah's Arc start joining as well. The male and female pair of the wolves, then the tigers, the bulls, the hawks, the gorillas, and finally, the lions.

There are six Spirits in the house with Sheeshal. "They are too strong, Sheeshal," Spirit Naruzu urges. He is a resident of one of the other houses at the Warbler Estates. "We cannot defeat them."

"I have waited too long for this moment. I cannot give up now," Sheeshal disagrees.

"You will have to wait a while longer," Another Spirit, Raki, joins in.

"But the human morals in this society have never been lower. This is the perfect time to strike," Sheeshal tries to rally up his troops.

"As long as there are humans like them protecting their people, we cannot win." Naruzu points towards the group, walking towards the house "But there are less and less people learning their skills . . . we will have another opportunity."

"The opportunity is now. If we can defeat them, this whole place will be ours," Sheeshal persists.

"Sheeshal, don't lose the war over a battle. Our time will come, but it's not now," Naruzu tries to convince the Spirit.

"I will not give up!" Sheeshal shouts.

They all look out the window to see an army approaching.

"Well, then, this could very well be good bye, Sheeshal." One by one, the five Spirits slowly make their escape, leaving Sheeshal alone by himself.

It isn't long before Sheeshal is surrounded. He knows very well that this is not a battle he can win, but he has too much anger. He tries to attack Ahsan first and is pushed off by Abu Zan. Then he heads to the man reciting the verses from the Bible, but the Spirits of Noah's Arc would not let him come near. He turns his attention towards Rabbi Yannis, but Rabbi Yannis is prepared and already angry for what Sheeshal has done to his friend. He throws holy water toward Sheeshal and Abu Zan grabs his shoulders, keeping him in place, so he cannot move out of the way. The bottle explodes and falls on Sheeshal, and he screams in pain as Abu Zan throws the quickly evaporating Spirit across the room in the direction of Amir. Amir, oblivious to what exactly is going on, inhales the evaporating Sheeshal.

Father Montessori runs over to Amir.

"Why did you do that?" he asks, looking in horror at Ahsan and Abu Zan.

"What? Sheeshal is gone! We killed him," Ahsan replies without any concern.

Father Montessori turns his attention to Amir.

"Are you okay, son?" he asks, rubbing his chest.

"Yes, I am fine, Father . . . why do you ask?" Since Amir can't see the Spirits, he still isn't sure what happened.

"Nothing. I just want to make sure you are okay," Father Montessori responds with concern.

"Is he gone?" Amir asks, looking around.

"Yes. It worked. He won't be bothering you anymore," Rabbi Yannis confirms.

Afi Bhai

38

 Sharon walks into the master bedroom to find Amir still laying in bed.

"Are you gonna get out of bed today?" she asks in a frustrating voice. Amir just grunts from underneath the covers. "I don't understand what's going on . . . you have been in bed for the last five days."

"I told you, I don't feel good," Amir responds in anger.

"You need to get out of bed, move around, and gain some strength," Sharon tries to reason with Amir. But all Amir hears is a voice in his head, "Gain some strength..."

"You are right..." Amir pulls the covers off and sits up. "I am gonna take a shower and get ready."

"Great! We have that meeting with the EMR company," Sharon reminds him, relieved that Amir is up.

"I'm not going to work. I have some things to do. You can reschedule it or handle it yourself," Amir says with annoyance.

"What do you mean?" Sharon asks, confused. "What do you have to do?"

"THINGS!" Amir almost yells back at her. "I . . . don't have to tell you shit!" He has much anger and hate in his voice.

At that, Amir walks into the bathroom. And the voice in his head keeps repeating, "gain some strength . . . gain some strength. . . gain some strength. . ."

END

CPSIA information can be obtained
at www.ICGtesting.com
Printed in the USA
LVHW031019090419
613499LV00012B/222/P